IB
CATALAN PE Secret
Catalanotto, Peter.
The secret lunch special /
LAT 1070917925

Chapter books from
Henry Holt and Company:

The Secret Lunch
Special

2nd-Grade Friends

The Secret Lunch Special

Peter Catalanotto
and Pamela Schembri

Henry Holt and Company ✳ New York

Henry Holt and Company, LLC
Publishers since 1866
175 Fifth Avenue, New York, New York 10010
www.henryholtchildrensbooks.com

Henry Holt® is a registered trademark of
Henry Holt and Company, LLC.
Text copyright © 2006 by Peter Catalanotto and Pamela Schembri
Illustrations copyright © 2006 by Peter Catalanotto
All rights reserved.
Distributed in Canada by H. B. Fenn and Company Ltd.

Library of Congress Cataloging-in-Publication Data
Catalanotto, Peter.
The secret lunch special / Peter Catalanotto and Pamela Schembri.—1st ed.
p.   cm. — (Second-grade friends; bk. 1)
Summary: Second-grader Emily's memorable day includes a new school bus,
a forgotten lunch bag, a special cafeteria meal, and a new friendship.
ISBN-13: 978-0-8050-7838-1 / ISBN-10: 0-8050-7838-X
[1. Schools—Fiction. 2. Food—Fiction. 3. Friendship—Fiction.]
I. Schembri, Pamela. II. Title. III. Series.
PZ7.C26878Sec 2006   [E]—dc22   2006002374

First Edition—2006 / Book designed by Amelia May Anderson
Printed in the United States of America on acid-free paper. ∞

1 3 5 7 9 10 8 6 4 2

*For Diane Alder, Michael Testani, and Joe Rutz,
in gratitude for the kindness and
encouragement you gave my daughter*
—P. C.

To my Emily
—P. S.

2nd-Grade
Friends

The Secret Lunch
Special

Contents

Chapter 1

★

The Little Bus

Emily did not like to sit near the front of the school bus. Those seats were saved for the kindergarteners.

She did not like to sit near the back of the bus. Those seats were taken by the big kids.

Emily always sat seven seats behind the bus driver, by herself. She liked to look out the window.

For the first two weeks of second grade,
that's where Emily sat. Then, everything
changed. Emily and her mom watched as
a different bus stopped in front of their
house. A small bus.

Emily looked at her mom and wrinkled her nose.

The bus door popped open.

"Good morning! You must be Emily. I'm Ann, your new bus driver." Ann's voice was loud and cheerful, like a TV show for babies.

"Where's the other bus?" Emily asked.

"This is a *new* bus," Ann said. "It's just for children who live on Mountain Road. It will be safer in the snow." Ann had a big smile and big teeth. Emily could see all of her gums.

Emily knew her road got a lot of
snow but not enough for a small bus.
She picked up her violin and book bag.
"Watch your step, sweetie," said Ann.

Emily sighed and stepped on the
bus. Her mom followed and peeked
inside the bus.

"It's so cute!" said her mom.

"Mom!" Emily whispered. Two fourth-grade boys were staring. Emily's mom waved to them. "Hi, Adam! Hi, Chandler!" "Mom!" she whispered again.

"Emily, do you have your violin music?"
"Yes, Mom."
"Your lunch?"
"Yes, Mom."

Emily's mom handed her a sweatshirt.
"You might need this at recess."

"Okay, Mom."

"Bye, Emily. Bye, Adam. Bye, Chandler.
Bye, Ann. Bye, little bus!"

"MOM!" said Emily.

The door closed and the bus pulled
away.

Chapter 2

Ice Cream Day

Emily did not like her new seat.

She was only one seat away from the fourth-grade boys.

She was only one seat away from the kindergarteners.

At the next stop, Little Louie got on. Little Louie never had a tissue. He always needed one.

Emily turned toward the window. There was a squished bug. It was huge.

Emily did not like her new seat at all.

She closed her eyes and tried to think of something fun. She remembered it was ice cream day. Every Monday, her mom gave her money for ice cream.

Emily pulled out her shiny black lunch bag. She put it on the seat. It was covered with jewels. She smiled. She loved the way it sparkled. The money was in the front pouch. She would get an ice cream sandwich.

The bus made two more stops and
then pulled up to the school.

Emily picked up her violin.

She picked up her book bag.

She picked up her sweatshirt.

She went to her class.

Mr. Marvin, her teacher, was talking on the phone. Vincetta Louise was drawing on the chalkboard. *That* was not allowed. Vincetta Louise was not a very good listener.

Emily went to her cubby. Vincetta
Louise followed her.

"See my new lunch bag?" asked
Vincetta Louise.

Of course I do, thought Emily. It
was right in her face.

"It matches my shoes," said Vincetta Louise. Her shoes and her bag were pink and purple, with lots of glitter. Even the inside of the bag had a big silver zipper.

"Neat," said Emily. "Look at mine." She reached in her book bag, but there was no lunch. Her stomach sank.

"Well?" asked Vincetta Louise. She checked the sparkle clips in her long red hair.

Emily felt sick.

"Well?" Vincetta Louise tapped her foot.

"It's not here," Emily said. "I left it on the bus."

"Well! *You're* going to get a ticket
from Mr. Marvin."

"A ticket?" Emily asked. Her mom
once got a ticket for driving too fast.

She'd had to pay money because of the ticket. Was Emily going to have to pay money, too?

"Yep! A *ticket*," said Vincetta Louise. She snapped her bag shut and walked away.

Chapter 3

*

The Ticket

Emily could not stop thinking about the ticket.

The class said the Pledge of Allegiance.

Emily thought about the ticket.

Mr. Marvin took attendance.

Emily worried about the ticket.

Mr. Marvin took lunch count.
"Raise your hand if you are buying
lunch today."

Seven hands went up.

"Raise your hand if you brought
lunch from home."

Twelve hands went up.

"That's only nineteen," Mr. Marvin said. "Who didn't raise a hand?"

"Emily didn't!" yelled Vincetta Louise.

"Thank you, Vincetta Louise," said Mr. Marvin. "Please raise *your* hand and use an inside voice when you speak."

"Could you call me Vinni? Please?"

"Could you raise your hand, *please*?" asked Mr. Marvin. "Now, Emily, are you buying lunch or did you bring your lunch?"

"Neither," said Emily. "Both."

Mr. Marvin waited.

Emily explained, "I had my lunch, and money for ice cream, but I left them on the bus."

"Okay," said Mr. Marvin. "I have to give you a ticket."

Vincetta Louise mouthed, *Told you*.

"Please don't give me a ticket! I won't do it again!" Emily promised.

"Emily, it's just a charge ticket," said Mr. Marvin. He handed Emily a slip of paper. "Give this to the lunch lady. She'll give you a lunch. Tomorrow, you can bring her the money."

"I'm not in trouble?" asked Emily.

"Hardly," said Mr. Marvin.

Vincetta Louise laughed. Mr. Marvin ignored her. Emily decided she would never talk to Vincetta Louise again.

Chapter 4

★

Aunt Nancy

At lunch, Emily hid her ticket in her hand.

A lunch lady gave her a tray.

Emily saw a pile of meat. It had a strong smell. Emily turned her head. She put down the tray.

"What's the matter?" asked the lunch lady. "Everybody likes Sloppy Joes!"

Emily didn't.

She didn't like sloppy *anything*.

Sloppy handwriting.

Sloppy bedroom.

Sloppy food.

She wrinkled her nose.

"Pick a pear from the bowl," said the lunch lady, "and you'll need a milk."

All the pears had brown spots. Emily took a pear with only three brown spots. Then she took a carton of milk. The next stop was the ice cream freezer. She could see the ice cream sandwiches on top.

At last, thought Emily, *something I can eat*.

Vincetta Louise slid next to Emily. "You can't charge an ice cream," she said.

Emily put an ice cream sandwich on her tray.

"You can't! I'm telling you!"

"Well," said Emily, "I'm not listening to you. You don't know everything."

"You'll see," said Vincetta Louise.

Emily slid her tray to the register
and handed the lady her ticket.

"Sorry, no ice cream with a charge
ticket."

Emily closed her eyes.

Vincetta Louise whispered, "Told you!"

Emily lowered her head. Her voice trembled. "I don't want this food. I don't want that ticket. I can't eat this!"

"You have to eat, honey," said the lady at the register.

"I can't! The smell is making me sick!"

Vincetta Louise laughed. "Mrs. Mancini, she can't eat that stuff. Look at it! It's mystery meat."

"Vinni, shhh!" Mrs. Mancini said.

"Let Emily have the secret lunch special," said Vincetta Louise. "Just this once."

Mrs. Mancini smiled. She removed
the Sloppy Joe from Emily's tray,
reached under the counter, and gave
her half a plain buttered bagel.

"Could you eat *that*?" asked Mrs. Mancini.

"Yes! Thank you!" said Emily.

The two girls walked to their seats.

"How do you know about the secret lunch special?" Emily asked.

"Shhh!" Vincetta Louise looked around the cafeteria. She whispered, "Mrs. Mancini is my Aunt Nancy."

"Lucky!" said Emily.

"Shhh!" said Vincetta Louise. "Here.
Take half my ice cream sandwich."

"Thanks, Vincetta Louise," said Emily.
"Call me Vinni. We're friends now."

Chapter 5

A New Friend...Maybe

After lunch, the class went to art.

Emily sat next to Vinni.

"Today we will paint with fall colors," said the art teacher, Miss Culver. "Does anyone know the colors of fall?"

Emily raised her hand.

"Black and blue!" Vinni called out.

"Black and blue?" asked Miss Culver.

"Yeah," said Vinni. "Every time I fall, my knee turns black and blue!" Vinni laughed. So did Joey, Julia, and Janelle.

Emily frowned. Emily would never talk like that in school.

Miss Culver continued. "Today we are going to paint with *autumn* colors. I have red, orange, and gold paint."

Miss Culver covered each table
with newspaper. Emily saw a picture
of the new Sabrina doll.

"Look!" said Emily. "This is what I want for my birthday. Wow! Look at the list of stuff that comes with it!"

Vinni waited. "Well?"

"What?" asked Emily.

"READ IT!" shouted Vinni.

"Girls!" said Miss Culver. "Shhh!"

Quietly, Emily read to Vinni. "A mini makeup mirror, a hair dryer, a skateboard, and a boom box."

"Cool," said Vinni. "But her outfit would look much better like this."

Vinni drew Sabrina with a spaghetti-strap dress and high heels. She added a bandanna and sunglasses.

It's perfect, Emily thought.

Vinni turned to mix her autumn paints. Emily slipped the drawing in her pocket.

Emily had a violin lesson after school. At the end of the day, her dad was waiting to pick her up. They walked to the car. A loud horn beeped three times.

"Emily! Yoo-hoo! Emmy!"

Emily looked back. It was Ann, the bus driver, waving a sparkling black lunch bag.

"Is that yours?" asked her dad.

"Yes," said Emily.

"I didn't know you rode a little bus."

"It's for the snow," said Emily.

Her dad looked around. "Oh."

Emily thanked Ann, took her bag,
and climbed into the back of the car.

"Toodle-loo!" called Ann. "See you
in the morning!"

Emily's dad looked at her in the rearview mirror. "What did you do for lunch today?"

"I got a ticket," said Emily.

"They called the police?" her dad laughed.

"Funny, Dad. A ticket to charge lunch."

"What else happened today, honey?"

Emily took Vinni's drawing out of her pocket. She showed her dad.

"This is what I want for my birthday."

"Cool," said her dad. "Did you draw this?"

"No. Vinni did."

"Who's Vinni?"

"She's my new friend . . . I think."